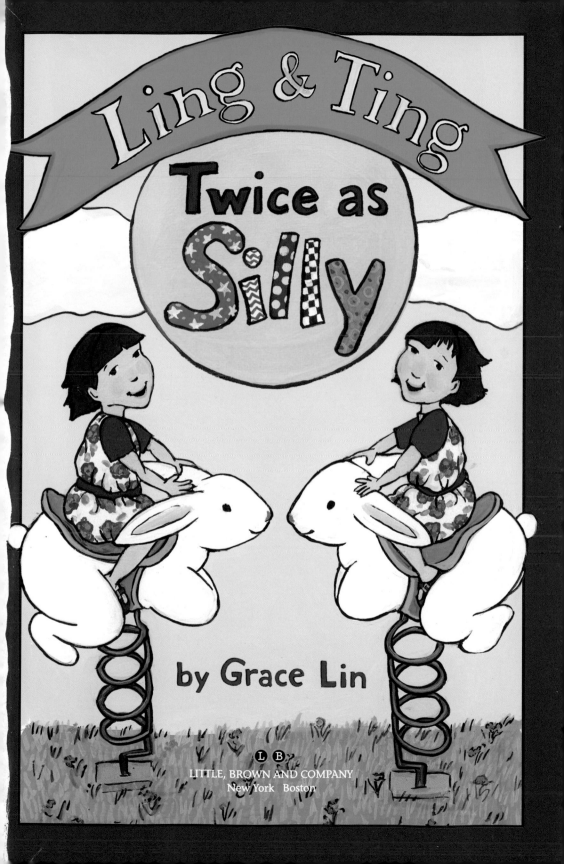

Ling & Ting

Twice as Silly

by Grace Lin

L B
LITTLE, BROWN AND COMPANY
New York   Boston

Double thanks to twins Emily and Olivia

Little, Brown and Company

Hachette Book Group
1290 Avenue of the Americas, New York, NY 10019
Visit our website at lb-kids.com

Little, Brown and Company is a division of Hachette Book Group, Inc.
The Little, Brown name and logo are trademarks of Hachette Book Group, Inc.

The publisher is not responsible for websites (or their content) that are not owned by the publisher.

First Edition: November 2014

Library of Congress Cataloging-in-Publication Data

Lin, Grace, author, illustrator.
Ling & Ting : twice as silly / by Grace Lin.—First edition.
pages cm
Summary: "Identical twins Ling and Ting like to be silly, tell jokes, and laugh together"
— Provided by publisher.
ISBN 978-0-316-18402-1 (hardcover)
[1. Twins—Fiction. 2. Sisters—Fiction. 3. Play—Fiction. 4. Chinese Americans—Fiction. 5. Humorous stories.] I. Title. II. Title: Ling and Ting, twice as silly. III. Title: Twice as silly.
PZ7.L644Liq 2014
[E]—dc23
2013041479

10 9 8 7 6 5 4 3 2 1

SC

Printed in China

6 Stories

Ting is in the garden.

"What are you doing?" Ling asks.

"I am planting cupcakes," Ting says.

"Ting!" Ling says. "You cannot plant cupcakes."

Ting digs a hole. She puts in a cupcake.
She covers the hole.

"See!" Ting says.
"I can plant cupcakes."

"Ting!" Ling says. "Cupcakes will not grow.
Cupcakes are not seeds. Seeds grow."

"I will try anyway," Ting says.

Day after day, Ting weeds and waters
her garden.

Ting waits, but nothing grows.

"Ling," Ting says, "you are right. I will not have a cupcake garden. Cupcakes will not grow."

"Cupcakes are not seeds," Ling says. "Seeds grow."

"Are beans seeds?" Ting asks.

"Yes," Ling says. "Beans are seeds."

"Good," Ting says. "Then next I will plant
jelly beans."

Ling is at the table. She has a
paintbrush and a can of red paint.

"What are you doing?" Ting asks.

"I am painting my toys red," Ling says.
"Red is a lucky Chinese color. I want my
toys to be lucky. Do you want to paint?"

"Yes," Ting says. "I want to paint."

"You can paint now," Ling says. "I will get more paint."

"What should I paint?" Ting says.

"Paint everything," Ling says. "I will be back soon."

Ting likes to paint. She likes to paint fast. When Ting paints, the paint splashes. It splashes on Ting.

When Ling comes back, Ting is covered with paint. Ling laughs hard.

"Ting!" Ling says. "I said 'Paint everything'! I did not say 'Paint everyTING'!"

Ling and Ting are at the playground.
They are playing on the swings.

"How high can you swing?" Ting asks
Ling.

"I can swing higher than a tree,"
Ling says.

"You can?" Ting asks. "Which tree?"

"Any tree," Ling says.

"Any tree?" Ting asks. "A tree that is taller than a giraffe?"

"Yes," Ling says.

"A tree that is taller than a building?"
Ting asks.

"Yes," Ling says.

"A tree that is taller than a mountain?"
Ting asks.

"Yes," Ling says.

"A tree that is higher than the clouds?"
Ting asks.

"Yes," Ling says.

"A tree that goes into outer space?" Ting says. "A tree that is higher than the moon? A tree that is as high as the stars?"

"Yes," Ling says. "Yes. Yes."

"Okay," Ting says. "Show me how you can swing higher than a tree."

"I am doing it right now," Ling says. "We both are."

"We are?" Ting asks. "How?"

"It is easy to swing higher than a tree," Ling says. "A tree cannot swing."

"Look up there," Ting says. "There are apples. I want to eat them. Let us pick them."

"The apples are too high," Ling says. "We cannot climb that high."

"A monkey can climb that high," Ting says. "Let us get a monkey! A monkey will get us an apple."

"A monkey?" Ling asks. "How will we get a monkey?"

"We will go to the zoo," says Ting. "We will take a monkey from a cage."

"The cage will be locked at the zoo," says Ling. "Only the zookeeper has a key."

"A penguin will sneak the key for us," Ting says. "We will train a penguin to get the key."

"A penguin?" Ling asks. "How will we train a penguin?"

"We will feed the penguin a fish," Ting says. "Penguins will do anything for fish."

"We do not have any fish," Ling says. "How will we get a fish?"

"We will catch one," Ting says. "All we need is a worm."

"Where will we get a worm?" Ling says.

"We can get a worm in an apple,"
Ting says.

"Ting!" Ling says. "It is an apple we want! We do not want an apple for a worm! We want an apple to eat!"

"But how will we get one?" Ting says.

Ling climbs down.

"Come with me!" Ling says. "I know how we will get apples."

Ling brings Ting to the store. They buy
many apples.

Ling and Ting are reading books together.

"Ting," Ling says, "this book says some twins are special."

"Are we special?" Ting asks.

"Special twins can read minds," Ling says.

"Oh," Ting says. "Let us see if we are special."

"Okay," Ling says. "I will think of something. What am I thinking of?"

Ling looks at Ting. Ting looks at Ling. Ting scratches her head.

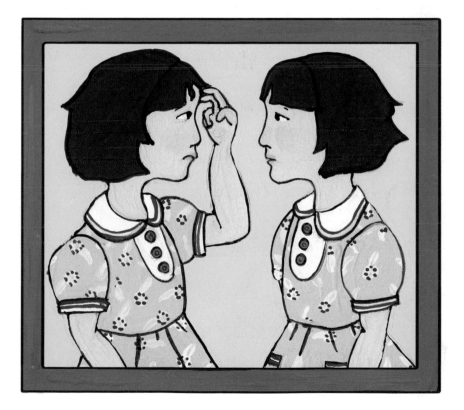

"It is something spelled with four letters," Ling says. "It begins with *b*."

Ling holds her book. Ting looks at the book.

"Are you thinking of a book?" Ting asks.

"Yes!" Ling says. "You did it! You read my mind! Now I will read your mind."

Ling looks at Ting. Ting looks at Ling.
Ling shakes her head.

"Nothing," Ling says. "My mind is
reading nothing."

"Ling! You are right!" Ting says. "I was thinking nothing!"

"Let us write a story," Ting says.

"Yes," Ling says. "But we will not write a silly story."

"Okay," Ting says. "It will not be silly."

Ling begins, "Ling and Ting were two girls...."

"Let us not be girls," Ting says. "Let us be rabbits!"

"Okay," Ling says. "Ling and Ting were two rabbits. One day they found an apple tree...."

LING   TING

Once there were two
~~girls~~ rabbits named
Ling and Ting.

They found an apple
a cupcake tree. The
cupcakes were at the
top of the tree.

"Not an apple tree," says Ting. "Let us make it a cupcake tree."

"Okay," Ling says. "One day they found a cupcake tree. They could not reach the cupcakes. They had to use a lucky red toy to jump."

"Yes," Ting says. "They jumped higher than the tree. They jumped into outer space!"

"Outer space?" Ling says.

"Yes!" Ting says. "Then Rabbit Ling said to Rabbit Ting, 'How will we get down?'"

Ling and Ting used their lucky toy. They jumped so high that they jumped over the tree.

"But you cannot talk in outer space," Ling says. "Outer space has no sound."

"Ling and Ting were special rabbits," Ting says. "They could read minds! So, with her mind, Ting told Ling to eat stars!"

They flew into outer space.
"How will we get down?" said Ling.
with her mind
Ting told Ling ∧ to eat the
stars.

"How could they eat stars?" asks Ling.

"The stars were really jelly beans," Ting says. "After Ling and Ting ate them, they were very heavy. They sank down to Earth."

After eating the jelly bean stars, Ling and Ting were very heavy. They sank back down to Earth.

On their way down, they picked some cupcakes. They ate the cupcakes for dessert. THE END

"What about the cupcake tree?" Ling says.

"They picked some cupcakes on their way down," Ting says. "That night, they had cupcakes for dessert after dinner. The end."

"Ting," Ling says, "I said we would not write a silly story."

"This is not a silly story," Ting says. "This is a very, very silly story!"

"You are right," Ling says. "It is very, very silly."

"Just like us," Ting says.

"Yes," Ling says. "Just like us."

★ ARTIST'S NOTE ★

The illustrations in this book were painted using Turner Design Gouache on Arches hot-pressed watercolor paper. While the color palette in *Ling & Ting Share a Birthday* was inspired by ice cream, the palette in this book was inspired by the bright blue summer sky and the late-ripening red strawberries of my first garden. —*Grace Lin*

★ ABOUT THIS BOOK ★

This book was edited by Alvina Ling and designed by Saho Fujii under the art direction of Patti Ann Harris. The production was supervised by Erika Schwartz, and the production editor was Christine Ma. This book was printed on 128-gsm Gold Sun matte paper. The text was set in StoneInfITC Medium, and the display type was hand-lettered by the author.

Perfect!

Read about our last haircut in "Ling and Ting: Not Exactly the Same!"